# Reverend Timms

**SIMON AND SCHUSTER**

Reverend Timms
St. Thomas Vicarage
Garner Bridge
Greendale

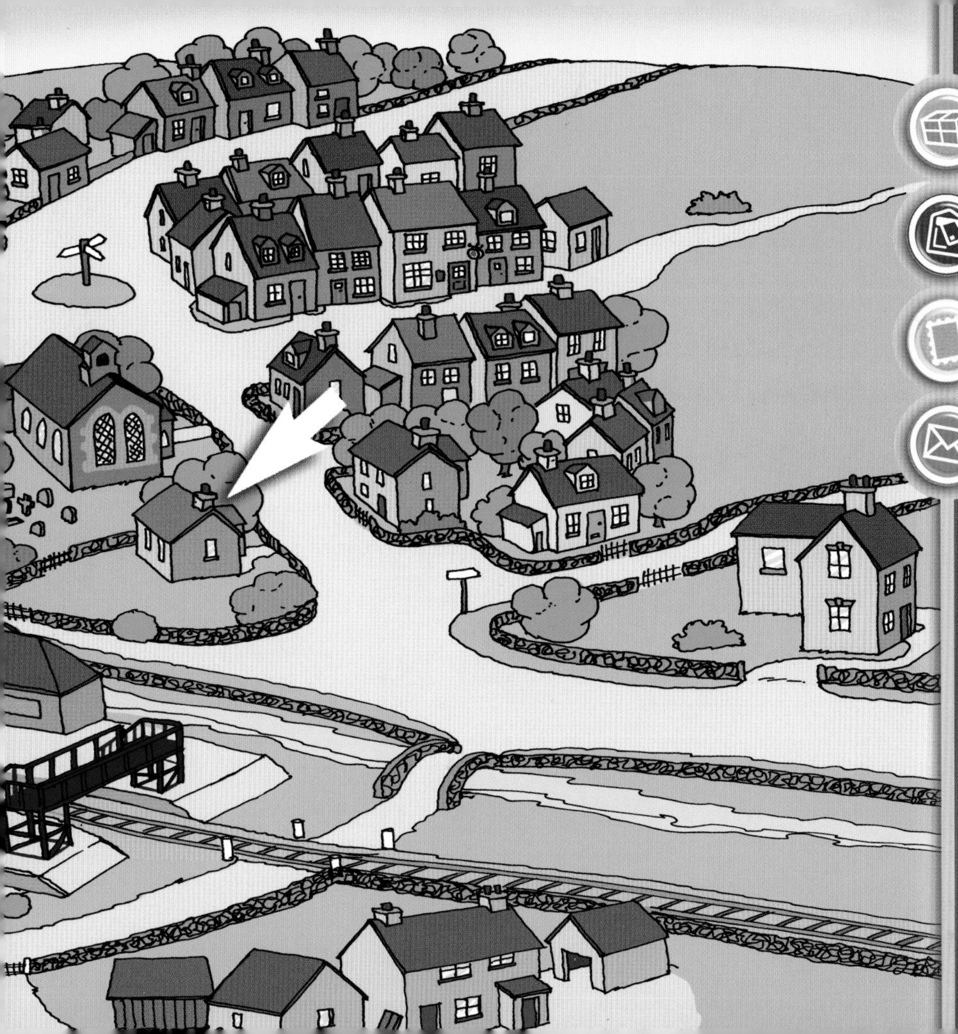

# GREENDALE

Come and say hello to Reverend Timms!

The Reverend looks after Greendale's Church, and all of its villagers! The kindly vicar can always be counted on to offer a helpful word to his friends. But once there was a time when he turned to his friends with a problem of his own...

Postman Pat was on his morning round, when he came across Reverend Timms doing press-ups.

"One... two..." puffed Reverend Timms. "Morning, Pat! Three..."

"Don't often see you in a tracksuit, Reverend," smiled Pat.

At first, the Reverend was a bit too red to speak.

"Are you alright?" asked Pat.

"I'm in training, Pat," Reverend Timms explained. "For a sponsored run."

The Reverend pointed up to a hole in the church steeple. "I need to raise enough funds to get it repaired, Pat."

"It'll need to be done before winter sets in," nodded Pat.

Jess nudged the Reverend's tracksuit pocket with his nose until a sponsor form dropped out.

"Good idea, Jess," said Pat. "We'll sponsor you, Vicar!"

"Oh, bless you," beamed Reverend Timms.

The Reverend was a bit tired by the time he started his weekly bell-ringing class.

Pat, Ajay, Ted and Julia were taking turns at pulling the bell rope.

"Do you want to ring the bell now, Vicar?" asked Ted.

"I'll just watch you for a while," said Reverend Timms. "I think I may have over-done the press-ups."

"Don't hurt yourself," warned Julia. "Ooohh!" she suddenly cried.

Everyone rushed over to Julia. "It's my hand!"

Reverend Timms fetched the first aid box, while Pat sat Julia down on a pew.

"Looks like a bee sting," said Pat.

Ajay scratched his head. "What would a bee be doing in here?"

"I think our answer's up there," announced Ted.

The most enormous beehive they'd ever seen was nestling in the church belfry.

Reverend Timms raised his eyes to heaven. "The bees must have buzzed in through the hole in the roof."

"The problem is going to be getting them back out again," said Pat.

"I'm going to have to do a lot more fundraising to cover the bill for that now," sighed the Reverend.

"No you won't, Vicar," said Ted. "I can get those little fellows out."

Ted headed off to his shed. An hour later he was back, loaded with a ladder, a hosepipe, a pair of bellows and a box of matches.

"Righto," said Ted. "First, we need to build a bonfire."

"Pat and I will find some wood," offered Ajay.

The Reverend whispered a little prayer and then mucked in to help too.

Ted fixed the hosepipe to the bellows and then set the ladder against the damaged bell tower.

"Hold the hose above the bonfire, Pat!" he called down.

"Got you!" cried Pat. Everyone watched as the smoke was sucked up the hosepipe and gently blown into the hole in the roof.

"Praise the Lord!" cheered Reverend Timms. "The smoke is making the bees sleepy."

The sleepy hive was carefully lifted down from the belfry.

"What shall we do with it now?" said Ajay.

The Reverend looked thoughtful. "Well, I am here to care for all creatures great and small..."

"What are you thinking, Vicar?" asked Pat.

"If we work together to build a hive, I'll give the bees a home in my garden."

Reverend Timms made the perfect beekeeper. He'd even learnt how to make jars of honey to sell in Mrs Goggins' post office.

"Your honey's sold out again, Vicar," smiled Pat one morning.

"I've been truly blessed!" smiled the Reverend. "Now we can afford to get the roof fixed."

"So no more sponsored runs?" asked Pat.

"Oh yes! But thanks to my friends, the funds can go to another good cause – sports equipment for Greendale Primary..."

**SIMON AND SCHUSTER**

First published in 2006 in Great Britain by Simon & Schuster UK Ltd.
Africa House, 64-78 Kingsway, London WC2B 6AH
A CBS COMPANY

Postman Pat® © 2006 Woodland Animations, a division of Entertainment Rights PLC.
Licensed by Entertainment Rights PLC
Original writer John Cunliffe
From the original television design by Ivor Wood
Royal Mail and Post Office imagery is used by kind permission of Royal Mail Group plc
All Rights Reserved

Text by Mandy Archer © 2006 Simon & Schuster UK Ltd
Illustrations by Baz Rowell © 2006 Simon & Schuster UK Ltd

ISBN 1416916490
EAN 9781416916499
Printed in China
1 3 5 7 9 10 8 6 4 2